The Tin Forest

Written by Helen Ward   Illustrated by Wayne Anderson

templar publishing

There was once a wide, windswept place,

near nowhere and close to forgotten,
that was filled with all the things
that no one wanted.

Right in the middle was a small house,
with small windows,
that looked out on other people's rubbish
and bad weather.

In the house
lived an old man.

Every day he tried to tidy away the rubbish,

sifting and sorting,

burning and burying.

And every night
the old man
dreamed.

He dreamed he lived in a
jungle full of wild forest animals.
There were colourful birds,
tropical trees, exotic flowers,
toucans, tree frogs
and tigers.

But when he awoke,
his world outside was
still the same.

One day something
caught the old man's eye
and an idea planted itself in his head.

The idea grew roots and sprouted.
Feeding on the rubbish,
it grew leaves.

It grew branches.

It grew bigger and bigger.

Under the old man's hand,
a forest emerged.

A forest made of rubbish.
A forest made of tin.
It was not the forest of his dreams,
but it was a forest just the same.

Then one day across the windswept plain
the wind swept a small bird.
The old man spilled crumbs from his
sandwiches onto the ground.
The bird ate the crumbs and perched
to sing in the branches of a tin tree.

But the next morning the visitor
was gone.

All day the old man
walked through the silence
and his heart ached with emptiness.

That night, by moonlight,
he made a wish...

In the morning the old man
woke to the sound of birdsong.
The visitor had returned and,
with him, his mate.

The birds dropped seeds from their beaks.
Soon, green shoots broke
through the earth.

Time passed. The song of birds mingled
with the buzzing of insects
and the rustle of leaves.

Small creatures appeared, creeping
amongst the jungle of trees. Wild animals
slipped through the green shadows.

There was once a forest,
near nowhere and close to forgotten,
that was filled with all the things
that everyone wanted.

And in the middle was a small house
and an old man who had toucans,
tree frogs and tigers in his garden.